WENDING

a verse novella

By Bel Hawley

First published in 2025 by ECG Press
www.ecgpress.com

ISBN
Paperback: 978-1-7636892-1-3
Ebook:978-1-7636892-2-0

Layout and typesetting: ECG Press

Cover design: Halli Starling | https://hallistarlingbooks.com/

Please send all permission queries to info@ecgpress.com

A Cataloging-in-Publication entry for this book is available from the National Library of Australia.

For C & J

contents

the river sand is black

1.

i say i want a stake
in the business
a role

until i am banished
there
                here

          they don't want his widow

so they send me to this river
where footprints pockmark the ground beside it

                    like a moonscape

i follow   baffled

i am hindered not
by the extraterrestrial

    ground

as a family
we were only together a short time

and the river sand is black
beneath

2.

my feet kiss the water
press against the sweeping surface
(scrying obsidian)
the mix of water and cool air
shocking them red

bending forward i
move my hands down
over my calves
rubbing the droplets of dirt off
before submerging
plunging under
to remove the grime

3.

i'm martyred here
on the crushing rocks
i'm both succumbing
and indifferent
until my body

unable to cope with the pain
sinks sideways
the few sharp stone pieces
still imbedded
in my soles
ticking away

4.

there is valiance in this edge
of the natural world
a frontline of wilderness

beckoning

the manifest with green writing

earlier when i was above the ravine
wind battering from every direction

i felt them begin to hover back
retreat before they even said they were going

these two men had brought me here
we'd cried through all kinds of weather

as they explained my work around hand gestures
– through absurdity

and while they seemed nice enough in their own way
their beguiling platitudes

landed strangely
as everything cut off abruptly

it was as if we materialised here
with never-ending nature in all directions

i have no solid memories of before
just hazy flashes of rain and instructions

and of how the otherwise engulfing
won

magnified by the overwhelm of trees
at the lip of where we stood

i said i hadn't mentioned my late husband
and their body language changed

shifted awkwardly towards
equipment and supplies – a camp roll

towards asking me if i needed a hand
while i shivered through several loads

offering to bring back a real bed in afterthought
unsure if there was one down in the house below

handing me a frequency number
and an emergency code

they told me: *journal everything* (including the trip)
as if i could remember the day's developments

the manifest with green writing appearing
or this man who felt regret

i turned towards the passway – a cement
squared off U (very modern) pointed out to me

continued down in grey shadows
until i saw the river in the slim ravine

long green stalks and flowers that looked like tiny
bells sprouting at the base

the pungent white-floral hitting
as i descended into its heady thickness

the smell then escaping
like a watery spring you know can't last

as they disappeared into the background
in my descent

i tried not to look back

recessed here

in the wake of the first day
my proximity to the water
was disconcerting
until i realised this is nocturne
glowing with possibilities
and i leaned into the sorrow
my invisible walls
keeping me calm
like the shrieking each morning

i uncover the cellar
rust coating my fingertips
shout down into it
listen
to the returning call
as it bounces
first to me
then up into
the dark

recessed here
you only see darkness
even on the brightest day

like you were never

i don't see how that can be true
we threw down like warriors
and the death certificate reads
like you were never

in this giant cavernous expanse
i refute the implication with fervor
and summer on the front porch
of this cool winding world
with my hair in my hands

ever since the words came
i've been wading further in hopes of new life
i fear once the birds leave there will be
nothing but an awful silence and the wait
and the wading

centaurides

in this strange place there is a
mural on the wall
with centaurides

their cascading manes
and glossy sunlit coats
remind me of the café
in northcote

where i once met an old friend
and changed her baby
just outside the kitchen

(much to everyone's disgust)

we moved deep inside
away from the sun after that
but still her hair shone
waist length

as she bent in to remove the evidence
plucking the nappy up and
placing it in a reusable bag
i knew would not be reused

we discussed our husbands
homes we had

homes we wanted

i never would have thought
that moment
would ever be on a path to this moment

the glossy blue tiles
and mythology themed décor
replaced by ancient canned foods
and mottled walls

oh the swift exchange
of one existence for another

there is a pace i have to keep

i set out early
something has been here during the night
and the crisp air is alive
        with the smell
of warm wet fur

i collect two new fungi samples
one near the stagnant
one near the rapids

sundays are not usually as
full as other days
i wrap my jumper around my waist
tie it at the front and walk

through undergrowth
through walls of branches
that are of no match
not completely

people don't know i grew up in denser bush than this
within a family who
didn't really see gender
until it appeared on the body

and my body didn't show

until i was well into my seventeenth year
a shock to both me and them

i had to learn a few things fast

my lungs are full
of the sting of breathing
there is a pace i have to keep

to take it further today
and still make it back

safely

when she first arrived by the river

at first she was
like a memory
 just out of reach
a fragment
that seemed to get
stronger
(her hair may have even changed colour
over the months i have been here)

she's non-descript
reminds me of someone
i knew when i was young
but who
i can't think
(maybe everyone i've ever known)
her arms like spindles
as she makes baskets in the
drizzle and haze
i saw her once
spinning wool
where the wheel came from
i do not know
nor do i know where the foot upon the pedal
has trod
regardless
they both disappeared
the woman and the wheel

like they'd never been
but they had
i came home from a hike once to
a rock placed on
a slate grey jumper
oversized
like it had been made
with
too much love

jumpers

the following morning
i bring the soft garment
to my nose
                inhale the lanolin

the cloying smell
reminding me of when i was young
of my nan's insistence
that if i was going to play near the fire
could i please wear wool?

i had one woollen dress as a child
that never lost the sour-milk scent
of paddock and yolk
until the day i landed
in a jack jumper nest
and was basted in onions as treatment

it's appropriate though
well-made
and with the seeping cold of the nights
having me almost on top of the fire
if i didn't need it so much
i'd be unable to trust something weaved in the
low gathering cloud

                        but for now i just put it on

living ordinary

the chill shouldn't bother me so
i'm not camping
in a dilapidated space
or living
unchecked
it's me broken down
in the everyday
living ordinary
in this white and coffee cream home
that *resembles*
home
like a terraced house
thin and unsqueezed
plucked and set here
by itself

losing hours

the problem
with the work i've been given
is that it often requires
making records
crossing things off

tedious to a point where i'm
weary

the pounding behind my right eye
preventing me from sleeping

as a teen i resented
running
rousing
waking

losing

hours

on the farm
in the shop my parents ran
at the markets
legs swinging as i sat on a seat too high
serving thieves mostly
as they all stole

when i couldn't concentrate
long enough
to catch them

had no idea what i'd do if i did

bleakly
i sit here amongst this
it's testing
toiling
devolving

it's pounding behind my right eye

losing hours

(skin off breasts)

crawling along
the kinds of paths
you can only scramble

where steep is clinging
to the walls of the earth

where you might slide
after
downwards
tearing up the front of your body
(skin off breasts)
abrasions on the belly button
that always stuck out too far
on your pelvic bone
your knees

where biting the soil
sinking
your lips into the grit
face and hair caked
with the crime of
surrender

and the possibility of smacking rock
instead of the give of dirt
where the possibility of teeth breaking

fingernails scraped to flesh
chin painfully holding

                         sideways on a ledge

might be the only anchor that saves you

gasping for breath

i'm in the corridor again
i say again
but each time it differs
almost always i'm running
desperate

                      to get to you

with some unknown knowledge

                                you're
just a corridor away

i pull myself back
in a hurry
gasping for breath

as if someone has been
holding me underwater

once again there is wilderness all around me
i wonder if i'm slipping

                      between realities
if there's a new present
i'm being plagued with

i hear her footsteps nearby

they lift me from the helpless feelings
of not being able to see you

there

                 she is

between the trees

i think i see her as a child
a patch over her eye
hair stuck in the
medical tape

is she jumping realities too?

pantomiming

in a crevice nearby
i test the tepid discard
sink deep in a natural bowl
carved out by the warm spring
cover myself completely
in the groundwater
until i'm
suspended in the silence
eyes following the walls
reaching up either side of me
touching what looks like crystal
looming in a deep hue
in the corner
the candle flames
are oddly pink in comparison

                            light
                                and shadow

pantomiming across

the wet foliage bleeds across my arm

1.

i take my compass from my backpack
and unwrap it from a soft cloth

it was given to me by my husband
for our 7th anniversary

antique and mechanical
fully functional yet not practical

the model before *the* model
bests anything i've used before

there's a spot i need to get to
a few days from here

i don't know if i'm supposed to leave
not for that long anyhow

the samples won't get taken
everything will be left

clustered and unattended in a box
in the corner of the room

labelled only to amuse me
as this won't be the first time i've neglected them

for weeks at a time
i've allowed spillage

routinely guessed
areas and dates for labels

guessed
my real work is to stay out of the way

2.

as i walk deeper into the thickness of the escarpment
my clothes offer little protection

the backpack sits heavily against the small of my back
and my drink bottle digs into my left rib

i examine the compass carefully
before i scramble further upwards

the wet foliage bleeds across my arm
the damp blurring all directions

i'm distracted by something in the distance
but i've forgotten my binoculars and it's too far to see

i tap at the face and follow the flickering hand
turn away finally in the too-late-today

i make a mental note to come again tomorrow
take a closer look in person

picture the colours of the different organisms
just feet from my neglected chores

quiet on the bench in the house
sealed and thirsty in plastic containers

always waiting for me to return home
waiting for me to pick them up again

restore them to their environment
bring them back to life and make them useful

someone called today

when i picked up the satphone
there was a tinny distance
to the conversation
that made me feel
more alone than before

the water is getting fiercer by the day
the rain now more than drizzle
so i collect wood
stack it inside
dry it out before the deeper winter comes
penetrates
everything with its chill

i've pulled the wardrobe away from the corner
to make a small cavity
a pit for the kindling
before i was afraid it would roll into the fire
anytime i was away

even now i check everything as i'm leaving
thrice the coals
candle wicks pinched wet between fingers
quickly run under taps

there is little correspondence from home
never the brothers

just a few words from the sister
i try not to think about
the one i once allowed myself to get close to

she tends to bear bad news
breaks things to me
things that almost
destroy me

the latest supply drop is happening today
                              so i spring forth
           making my way
upwards to
where i stand and
wait

watch
it appear
watch it appear so close to the edge
i almost need to hold my breath

weatherlogged

i think about the man who comes here
his demeanor and our exchanges
me with a box of film clearly labelled
jostling around loose
him lifting the lid and narrowing his eyes
him shuffling the box awkwardly
tucking it deep
under one arm
before handing me an invoice
pausing before giving me three more boxes
and an inflatable bed
(also boxed and pump included)
everything reluctantly handed over
in exchange for my work

i leave him a leather roll
filled with somewhat accurate
sketches of the terrain
i leave him
to photograph the weather logs quickly
with his phone
only transferring the records myself
after i return
he seems happy with the drafts
but asks after
more than my crude landscapes

the records he wants are
almost complete
secreted away
under a crumpled sheet
hidden
at the bottom of the bookshelf
i'm afraid
and deep down i know
my late husband's brothers
will insist i leave
if they realise i'm this close
to finishing

i dare not mention there's a woman here
    i'm reluctant to leave
i'm certain i'm mistaken
    i'm certain i'm not right

yesterday

while climbing over
the river rocks
at the bend
i slipped on the fluorescent
moss
fell and sliced the back of my thigh

getting back to the house was slow
and i didn't make it until the night
was at its darkest
and i couldn't see an inch in front of myself

i held my feet forward
tried not to get turned around
feeling the river bank the whole way
and estimating the distance
what would i do if i hurt myself?
     hurt myself worse?
i couldn't call an ambulance
not to here

as dawn spiked the narrow gully
the path behind me was obvious
so was the path before me
blood spidered down my calf
like tree roots

despair

everyone always tells me about my grief
you were so lost in the beginning   or
you handled it with such dignity

this humours me
because i didn't feel lost in the beginning
more despair

and dignity?

more wild guttural howls
from recesses of my body
i never knew existed

because they weren't there

not in presence
not on the phone
it was me in my own collapse mostly

the whole sham abandonment
not just by the dead
but by everyone else

what people didn't understand

the only substantial thing i brought with me
was a chair his parents gave me
purchased
in an old school auction
it's simply a walnut chair
easily carried to the side
by a child
a groove in its top to seat yourself
small
well made
though the wood is thin
his father is gone now too
although more recent
it feels like it was in the before
we'd talked about what would happen
when his father went
he told me he wouldn't cope
that i would have had to take over everything
what people didn't understand
is that
with work
i pretty much did everything behind
scenes anyhow
though
interestingly
i didn't know about this role
it's not really served me in the way
i expected it to

the role or the chair

on it – the chair – awkwardly
in a room of dusty otherness
sits a satellite phone
not calling
oblivious

in the bottom of my cup

your brothers have sent me to a place
where there are no tides

just seasons

it's been two years since you left
and i'm here
where the air is so cutting
it bites at your lungs

where i have no mirror
and clothes are fine
as long as they're not infested with bugs

and *i'm* fine
or i would be
as long as my hair would stop falling out

my periods ceased at some point
did i miss menopause?
did my body accept you were gone before i did?

i fly
            fit
        muscle-ripped and dripping with sweat
      in the heat

i am both the sanest i've ever been
and the least sane

my coffee dregs are hardened
in the bottom of my cup
i think about your grave
how it sits alone
without anyone visiting

you left and i left
and now we wait to see what happens

next

at some point
i learnt i can smell when it's too cold to swim

unpolluted

i cleared the walkway this week
hacked at the vines that
invade either side
of the steep
freeing the concrete
where there is a mold
growing steadily

it's so damp here
the mushrooms seem to unfurl overnight
and the fig milk drops
in the folds of the ancient tree
refuse to dry

i hoisted buckets of river water
onto my hip
and worked my way down
and across
through hours
of scrubbing

then sat in steadfast guarding

that night my
hands were so swollen
my work   unfinished
everything paused

but the heart of this place

i returned to the pumice and a nail brush
intermittently
scrubbing away
the furry blanket of
black slime
while looking occasionally at the jagged walls
extending
down river

the
                    gradient

                                colours

so unlike the walls
i reside within
expecting a smell
different to what pooled around me
all that remained was
the unpolluted scent of
wet sweet
earth

an unholy smell that taunts me
even when i think of it now
and though the smell i inhaled
took me to the underworld

it didn't seem to harm anything
just curdled at my feet
settled like a child

what would it take
for this place to completely disappear?
for me?

trees shoulder to shoulder

the further i go
into the bush
no matter where i am
i can hear water tumbling
even when i can't see it
i hear it
i feel soft spray on the wind
the water
is like nature's clock
seconds rushing over
the chitter of the animals awakening
and then falling silent
before a duality
of bats and birds
that sweep noisily
when it stops
it's like the ravine's
sucked them back in
or thrown them away
and the shadows they cast
in between
like the damned
in situ
are in reality
a silent audience
waiting
to see what i do next

ready to bear witness
to my failings
to those who govern them
trees shoulder to shoulder

close my eyes

on an unusually warm day
i put my striped towel down upon the black sand
and imagine i'm on a coastal beach

if i close my eyes
the hollow wind fluting through the afternoon
could be mistaken for whispers

if i raise my hands
close my eyes   really reach
i can almost feel resistance

little warning

it's been a while now
since i turned from the land to the river
since i'd run as far as i could into the bush
between supply runs
pushing myself to the edge for the most
diverse pictures
making it back sometimes
with no time to spare
scratched
and with insect bites
travelling my body
like i'd caught something horrific

the man had dropped the kayak off
on his way to somewhere else
little warning
a few words through the satphone
half an hour beforehand
it opened up a whole new avenue of exploration
though he dropped it separate to the paddle

i had to wait weeks
using a stripped-down sapling instead
he'd said it was easier
to send the kayak ahead
by itself

but there was room in the crate

not plenty
but room
the boxes within boxes
tucked underneath
the same ones
that weren't mine
he was always racing
to deliver

still i was grateful

when he finally arrived again
                with my usual supplies
and handed me the shiny black rod
(strange as the kayak was wood)
like a prize
or a gift
something he was giving me personally
he'd instructed me on how to use it
i'd suffered the mansplaining quietly
took it from him with the right amount of 'gingerly'
he'd laughed and dangled a lifejacket before me
they were all laughing
but i'd grown up around water
had an uncle who was a skilled craftsman
who'd kept me in kayaks as a teen
who'd given me free reign and
any supplies i'd wanted

had taken me out on boats
so many boats
i knew what i was doing
it was just a kayak after all

my uncle had learnt his trade in america
there was a feature in our hometown paper
a massive two-page spread
showcasing the family
him
his sons
their wives

i'd married into an occupation too
one that i didn't create myself
one where i didn't work on a "floor"
inhaling particles
one where danger creaks above you

they don't acknowledge me
in the way my uncle does his daughters-in-law
even when my husband was alive
even when the will was read
but i know work
the work of my youth
the type of work that buries pain
deep in your hands
and back
so it can resurface

later

this kayak isn't perfect
it's not a work of art like my uncle's were
but it is functional

the rhythmic thwack of the blade
reminds me of
the sounds
of drawers opening

and closing

chasms

1.

feeling sure
albeit small
in this space
of walls climbing up
to settled fog

i sit in a small puddle
uncomfortable
as i paddle out

      feeling the force

   as the change comes

2.

a bend of my back
where the rapids

      discoloured from the scrum

look like lengths of mourning lace

the echoing cliffs
equal amounts windswept
 and wanting

bathed in shadow

1.

i hit the middle of the river
wide like a small fjord
on my kayak
in my red life jacket
i'm a fire ant on an autumn leaf

i never realised how big it was
even now
crisp and shady
with the sides looming
like two endless waves
leaning in
i don't think i'm seeing
the extent

i go in the opposite direction
at the end of the base camp
the water is fed
from a cave
channelled by
an intersecting
that rushes in

but to my knowledge
there is no ocean or sea near here

nothing large or extensive
other than
densely forested land
there could be anything underground though

for a while
i feel an invisible hand
pulling me back
holding onto the end of my kayak
near where i've packed my supplies
wrapped in plastic

i paddle deliberately
in the opposite direction
and once i'm past the bend
it's open
vast
an echoey natural passage
a chamber of still

2.

i've been on the river for hours
but travelled a lot further than expected
the river's flow moving me along
a child's paper boat
rapid and effortless in its navigation

i stop

stay in my cubby hole
the paddle solid across the tops of my thighs
pre-make knots
get my sketchbook out
map a little
nothing definitive today
loose estimates rather than marked terrain
just so i can decide
where i want to return

3.

i have met a fork
each of the river fronds
quiet
                        alike
each rescinding gradually
to the high walls of rock each side
i don't know when i'll be able to pull over again
so i travel to the edge
where everything's receded
step off
drag my backpack around
an apple falls out and rolls in the mud
i pick it up
wash it quickly
climb out awkwardly from my seat
there's little room to stand
between the dense brush

and the water
i can't bring my kayak in alongside me
so it flings out taut
like it's
baited and
ready to hook
perhaps already hooked

i grip the rope in my hand
place the paddle in the bay
of glossy wood
stand with a bush sticking me in the back
eat the apple
before the bruise sets in

then cautious

on the river i don't see her
but i feel her watching me
up on top of the cliffs
looking down
running alongside the river silent
bar the crackle of
leaves on the ground

she can reach great speeds
but can also stop
steady herself in an instant
alarmed
then cautious
i remember when a friend
from overseas
once visited
asked
you don't have anyone here?
i do
but they're far away

twin coves

upriver
it opens out briefly
twin coves either side
like something amphibian
puffed and bulging outwards

i keep to the centre
but watch below
it's quite shallow   calm
though something is darting and alive
underneath

the shadow of my kayak moves swiftly
creeping over the now ominous
river bottom
as expansive smooth boulders
become visible
heavy on the floor

i look around frantically
expecting the kayak to hit them
expecting the boulders
to take out the bottom
until i'm a story
an anomaly
a supposition
little more than discard

– a scuttled boat
never to be recovered

i'm scanning the coves either side
looking for signs of life
a glint of something that could be hers
– anyone's
but as the kayak batters through
as old as they are
as sunken
the boulders play softly
more like guides than adversaries

each shore sports
red algae
it looks denser
                    heavier

and slinks at the bottom
looks strangely like something was massacred here

and when the river gets too thin
it unexpectedly ceases

the older the better

i make camp

not far
it's sheltered
cold and hard
but i don't want to sleep at the coves
where the water hides things in plain sight
where the floor
is flat with low-lying threats
 – ladies in waiting
only seen
when visibility
is obscured

i think about the first day
when we stood overhead
my eyes following the water
as it curved around
through the ravine
then further
to its town house
hidden in the dark

i recall
the river flowing three
routes away from the bottom

the two on the outside
smaller
thinner
and clearly not as deep
almost see-through in places
(i must be near there now)

how it looked like
someone was
skinning something

how it looked like a reptile
shedding

on the way
before this great expanse
of mostly dark green
and dwindling waterways
was a lone mound
with a hollowed circle in its top
i remember pointing it out to the man
his laughter
they said you would make a mountain out of a mole hill
they did   did they?
he'd met my gaze briefly
they said lots of things
i'd turned away
i'd like a list of those
we'd travelled in silence for a while after that

eventually he'd laughed and said he was surprised i
wasn't more interested
in the river
like in its age
the older the better
now i wish i'd asked more questions

maybe there are more obstacles to come
maybe the boulders will lodge me somewhere
permanently
maybe this is it

i'll be forgotten
      abandoned on the river floor

            unable to

              come home

fixed

when i think
of work
        running errands
    sending emails

i have these thoughts about

                        speaking

to people
        in the lunchroom

i am
in one way fading
            unable to hang on

in another i'm here
fixed

it's just
there's anxiety

                there's
        (obvious)

    fear

all the time in the world

sometimes my husband and i
would hike to hidden places

he would marvel at the perfect beaches
gleaning with a single crescent of pure white sand

never did he understand
why they made me recoil

why i wasn't trusting of the water
unless the beach had a dirty foam crust

two-toned
like someone had taken a torch to it

where tiny shells gathered in hurried trenches
as if they knew something bad was coming

the stacks of seaweed
brown and cold

moving inwards at speeds we'd examine
like we had all the time in the world

the kidney shaped creature in my palm
the one i tucked down the back of his shirt

the running of our hands over cuttle fish
he said looked like wings

fanned out all over the beach as if
they were cast

from the making
of something bigger

from where he sits

in months to come
a man will perch above
the ravine
while winds push
distant reminders
that things can turn
with need
and rigidity

she hasn't arrived
again
hasn't met her obligations

he has supplies
but won't leave them
not this time
though he notes
the last boxes
have been removed

on another occasion he'd watched her running

wild

he can't even talk about what he'd seen
surely
he'd imagined it

he won't leave the supplies
this time
scanning the ravine from where he sits
he decides
it's not his job to report
if she's injured
it's not his job
to go down
to the base
he couldn't even tell you
what's down there

no one can

swansdown

madness
madness is not an instant thing
it's not standing tall
clutching a handful of swan necks
begging a man who couldn't care less
to take you home
it's not that same man
taking long enough to realise
the swan necks aren't snakes
or a bunch of calla lilies
you've carried out from the ravine
in a posy
holding them before you
in offering
like some medieval bride
or wanton widow
wild with grief
that they are empty of blood
but that you are covered in blood
you try to explain
they weren't meant to be
this isn't a place for swans
they have no use here
even as a food source
or even for feathers
swansdown

stuffing for your bedding
pillows
or the making of a powderpuff
because who
while wending through the middle of nowhere
through perilous ventures
would pick over
the fineness of a swan?
who would perform the letting?
who would
take that beautiful being in its arms
and commit it to the ground?

deep coffee cream trims

when i'd circled around the last time
the house looked
peaceful
its boards half
hidden
deep coffee cream trims
changed by decades
until they'd melded with the environment

if anything about this place
was set in stone
it was this house

i'm betting
it had always been here
as maybe i have been
or at least
will be

i drift through bees and grasshoppers

here the sun bears down
there's a wooded area
with a floor of flowers
that somehow
stretch into the river
colours muted in the long grass
as if holding everything back
and there beside it
i drift
through bees and grasshoppers
– a cacophony of low-key sounds –
knowing i should be somewhere else

spinning

time
as it passes
am i the only one left?
as here there isn't
anything
bar the hum in the distance
– the spinning of a wheel
and

                              her

acknowledgements

Thank you, ECG Press, for your never-ending patience and creative support during the publishing process.

Initially, this book was a quiet project, produced under the academic supervision of Deborah Hunn and edited by my friend, and fellow poet, Krystle Herdy. I'd like to thank you both for your kindness, poetic intuition, and considered advice.

All workshopping credit goes to Lena Pasqua and past classmates respectively. Pasqua, you are my fam!

Thank you to Iola Mathews and everyone I worked with at Glenfern Writers' Studios. While I didn't complete this project at Glenfern, I could not have produced it without my time there, learning how to lean into my writing.

Thank you also, Edwina and Susan, for your lovely words at such short notice. I appreciate you both more than you can imagine.

To Laurie, Lena, Shell, Gerlinda, and Les for their writerly comradeship after my husband passed. This, and anything I do beyond it, exists because none of you gave up on me.

Lastly, I'd like to thank my family and my late husband, Stuart. Here and not here, I feel your love and support always.

about the author

Bel Hawley is a writer with a special interest in female characters in contemporary fiction.

She holds a Bachelor of Arts from Curtin University, a Diploma of Professional Writing and Editing from NMIT, and is a former WoMentoring Project mentee and Glenfern Writers' Studios resident.

She has published in a variety of online and print journals, from *Westerly* to *The Victorian Writer*, and while primarily known for her short stories and literary fiction, it was her lived experience of widowhood that inspired *Wending*.

She resides in Victoria with her two children and a cat named Boots.